Skeleton Bones & Goblin Groans

POEMS FOR HALLOWEEN

Amy E. Sklansky

Illustrated by Karen Dismukes

HENRY HOLT AND COMPANY · NEW YORK

What Should I Be?

I've got to choose a costume.
Tomorrow's Halloween!
I think I'll be the spookiest
ghost you've ever seen.

Or . . .

a prickly pirate,
firefighter,
alien from space,

fearless cowboy,
Dracula,
detective on the case,

a baseball player,
lion tamer,
mummy wrapped up tight,

superhero,
wise old wizard,
goblin for a night.

Whatever I decide to be
(monster, hero, beast),
I want to get an early start
collecting all the treats!

Trick and Treat

A spider walks its web   on a dark Halloween night.

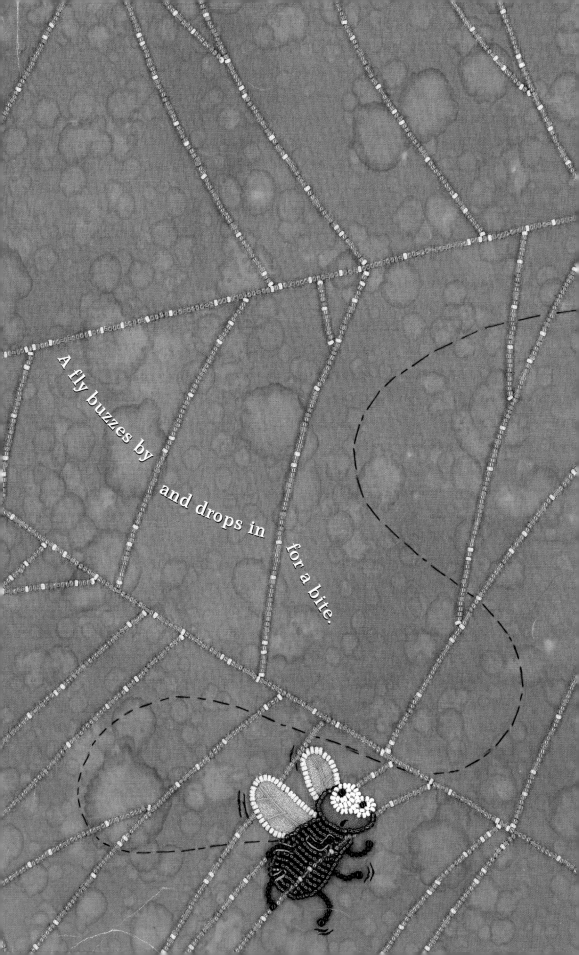

A fly buzzes by and drops in for a bite.

Halloween Wish

Wish I may,
wish I might

See
a skeleton
tonight,

Walking tall
with bones
of white,

Dancing in
the pale
moonlight.

Wish I may,
wish I might

Have my wish
come true
tonight.

Dinner Dilemma

Here come the trick-or-treaters
a-knockin' at my door—
just in time for me to dine
on two or three . . . or four.

Should I boil them with potatoes?
Make kid fricassee or stew?
Shish kebabs or oven roast?
Whatever shall I do?

But when I open up the door,
I fear they will have fled.
Then I guess I'll have to eat
some tuna fish instead.

House for Sale!

Two fireplaces. Eat-in-kitchen.

Atmosphere you'll find bewitchin'.
Lots of bedrooms. Space galore.
Slightly creaky hardwood floors.

Walk-in closets you can fill.
Stunning view atop a hill.
Asking price is very good.
In a lovely neighborhood.

All in all, just what you wanted.
(BY THE WAY, THIS HOUSE IS HAUNTED.)

A Broomstick's Life

Cooped up in this closet,
in the dark and in the dust,

I count the days till Halloween—
I feel like I might bust!

When that day arrives at last,
I knock upon the door.

Hooray! My witch, she sets me free.
I dance around the floor.

With a hop she climbs aboard,
we
Z o o m
across the sky.

'Round the moon and back again
we fly—my witch and I.

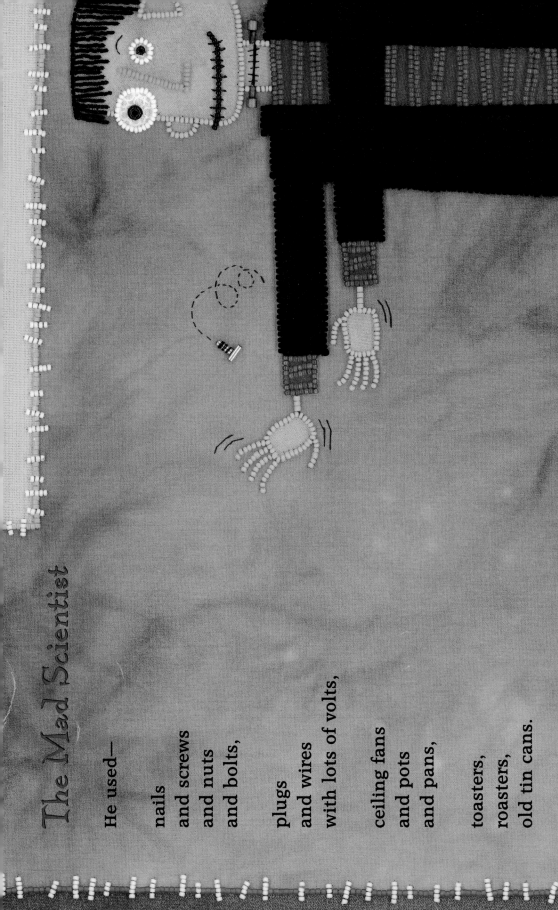

The Mad Scientist

He used—

nails
and screws
and nuts
and bolts,

plugs
and wires
with lots of volts,

ceiling fans
and pots
and pans,

toasters,
roasters,
old tin cans.

Then lightning somehow struck the tower
right before the midnight hour.

A spark! A sizzle!
A shock! A stir!

All parts at once began to *whirr*.

And at long last, his grand design
sprang to life. Meet

FRANKENSTEIN!

Cyclops

a cyclops is
like you
and I

except
he only has
one eye

centered
on his
broad
forehead

and if he
spies you

you'll
drop

d

e

a

d

The Bat

Upside down
hangs the bat.

There's really nothing
wrong with that.

Night Flight

Zip

zap

zoom

Bat flies across the moon.

Bip

bap

boom

Humming a silent tune.

Flip

flap

floom

Bat dives through evening air.

Dip

dap

doom

To land right in your hair!

Graveyard Dare

"Here to tap-dance on my tombstone?"
called a voice from underground.

"How did you know?" the young boy asked.
His eyes grew big and round.

"I know a lot about such things,"
the voice said with a sneer.
"I took the same dare just last week—
and now I'm buried HERE!"

Skeleton

Skull
mandible
sternum.

Radius
clavicle
fibula.

Ribs
scapula
pelvis.

Maxilla
humerus
tibia.

Two hundred six bones
make up me.
The same make up you,
but *mine* you can see!

Answering Machine Message

Hello, you've reached the Werewolves.
So sorry we're away.
The sky is clear, the moon is full—
call back another day.

Bobbing

Tub of water.
Apples red.
Time has come
to dunk your head.

Open up.
Take a bite.
Grab an apple—
hold on tight!

Mummy

entombed in a room
preserving dusty history
stranger from the past

Ghost

thin as a whisper
faded shadow
tremor of air

g
h
o
s
t

Grave

rocky pillow
bed of dirt and grass—
sleep forevermore

After Trick-or-Treating

Jawbreakers
candy corns
butterscotch
mints.

Bubble gum
lollipops
licorice whips.

I've just eaten
my trick-or-treat take.

All I have now
is one huge
tummy ache.

Jack O' Lantern

Jack o' lantern,
Jack o' light.

Jack o' darkness,
Jack o' night.

Jack o' scary,
Jack o' mean.

Jack o' lantern,
Halloween!

For my parents,
who let me read under the covers
—A. E. S.

For my favorite Halloween goblins—
Dani, Hunter, Clara, and Madeline
—K. D.

Henry Holt and Company, LLC
Publishers since 1866
115 West 18th Street, New York, New York 10011
www.henryholt.com

Henry Holt is a registered trademark of Henry Holt and Company, LLC
Text copyright © 2004 by Amy E. Sklansky
Illustrations copyright © 2004 by Karen Dismukes
All rights reserved.
Distributed in Canada by H. B. Fenn and Company Ltd.

Library of Congress Catalog Card Number: 2003022500
Full Library of Congress Cataloging-in-Publication Data available at
http://catalog.loc.gov/

ISBN 0-8050-7046-X / EAN 978-0-8050-7046-0
First Edition—2004 / Designed by Donna Mark
The artist beaded on canvas to create the illustrations for this book.
Printed in the United States of America on acid-free paper. ∞

10 9 8 7 6 5 4 3 2 1